Shh!
It's a Secret!

BY

JUS' VENUS

Order this book online at www.trafford.com
or email orders@trafford.com

Most Trafford titles are also available at major online book retailers.

Printed in the United States of America.

ISBN: 978-1-4269-5568-6 (sc)
ISBN: 978-1-4269-5569-3 (e)

Trafford rev. 02/07/2011

 www.trafford.com

North America & international
toll-free: 1 888 232 4444 (USA & Canada)
phone: 250 383 6864 ♦ fax: 812 355 4082

Dedicate To:

My God, the head of my life.
It is because of him and his blessed gift, I can use the imaginations of my mind to share with the world fantasies in my writings.

My Children, the loves of my life.
Thank you for encouraging your mother to fulfill a childhood dream.

My Life Long Friends, the main vein in all of this.
Your support, love, endurance to keep me at it and going when I just wanted to put it down. I just love you all. Thank you!

And to all the many fans of the King of Pop!
This 1 is 4 U.

Quote:

"It May Have Happened, It May Not Have Happened,

But It Could Have Happened"

Mark Twain

PROLOGUE:

Dear Minnie,

   Remember the times *when in our* **Childhood** *we felt* **Threaten** *by that* **Someone in the dark**, *that thing* **In the closet**, *making our hearts exceed* **2000 watts?** **I cant help it**, *a* **Hollywood tonight, Rock with you** *in the* **Morphine, Jam.** *Got me bouncing* **Off the wall, Bad** *and* **Dangerous.** *I didn't like the* **Man in the mirror** *which was just* **Another part of me.** *I had to stop and* **Beat it,** *I did.*

   I began my search for that **Liberian girl,** *and came across a* **Street walker,** *name* **Dirty Diana,** *a* **Heartbreaker, Who wanna be startin' somethin'.** *Whispering,* **Give into Me, Don't stop til you get enough.** *Because of her others came in hopes of invading my* **Privacy.** **Why you wanna trip on me? This is it.**

   As for us, we'd been **Just good friends** *trying to* **Heal the world,** *caring for* **The lost children.** *The ones who can hear the* **Earth song** *pleading* **Whatever happens, Don't walk away** *when others say* **They don't care about us. You are not alone,** *but know* **Heaven can't wait** *for you are the* **Break of dawn. Keep your head up** *the* **Monster** *only lives* **Behind the mask.**

   Now **This time around,** *you a* **PYT,** *became my* **Girlfriend, The lady in my life,** *Oh* **Baby be mine.**

ix

Through all my trials when **I can't make it another day,** *you're the* **Best of joy.** **The way you make me feel** *leaves me* **Speechless,** *gives me* **Butterflies. I like the way you love me. I just cant stop loving you.** *You helped ease the pain, so I can* **Fly away.** *What more can I say when its* **Human nature** *that draws me near to you.*

Having a new life enchanted me but it will be **Gone to soon.** *Not so far away was a* **Smooth criminal** *on the way* **Working day and night.** *The* **Tabloid junkies** *wont* **Leave me alone. Breaking news** *is all they ever say. They're like a* **Speed demon,** **Thriller** *preying on ones life. I* **Scream** *and even* **Cry** *to the* **Unbreakable** *truth of my* **Carousal** *life.*

But **One day in your life, a Stranger in Moscow** *will find you and* **Say Say Say, You rock my world.** *So do me this favor,* **Keep the faith** *of what may be because its never a* **Black or White,** *when your with* **Who is it** *that leaves you feeling* **Invincible.**

Much to soon *there will be* **Blood on the dance the floor,** *my journey coming to an end.* **Will you be there, Ben** *to catch a glimpse with* **Billie Jean?** *People say I* **Can't let her get away, The girl is mine.** *Taking control of the wheel* **She drives me wild.** *All not true.*

You are my life *a secret love.* **Who's Lovin' you,** *just* **Got to be there.** *So I* **Never can say good bye** *cause I* **wanna be where you are** *forever just to* **Hold my hand.**

Love Peter

Chapter 1

It's funny how certain things like a song, or a picture, or even a particular fragrance can remind you of a special time or event in your life. A memory of moments taking you back as long ago as childhood. Be it happy or sad, they some how have an uncanny knack of branding themselves in your memory forever. It was that way for me that afternoon on June 25th when, "It Should Have Been Me," could be heard playing over the intercom system at the Evansville Casket Factory warehouse in Manchester, Tennessee.

I'm Shelby Johnson aka Minnie. A nickname acquired by a long time best friend whom I simply called Peter. At 48 years of age and a single woman, I have been an over the road truck driver for 8yrs. And as of today, I have been out on the road this time for 3weeks non stop. Most of the loads came out of Evansville, so I was pretty much a regular driver coming through. This load for pick up is set to deliver in Los Angeles California, a 2 ½ to 3 day ride about 2,100 miles. The drive will be well worth it to be home for a few days.

The life of a truck driver can sometimes be a very lonely job but the reward of not having a boss or supervisor over your shoulder is fantastic. Depending on who or what company you work for, it can also be very financially rewarding. As for me, I worked for the family business and got a lot of fringe benefits. Most of the time, I just stayed on the road to occupy my mind from pressing issues at home.

It was a pretty hot day outside and I decided to sit in the cool warehouse near the back end of the trailer to watch the guys load. I always loved the aroma of the cedar, oak and mahogany woods that filled the air of the building. It was sectioned off; lids, cases, and interior linen on the right side. In the far rear, you could here hammering and saws cutting wood creating final resting beds. And to the left side on the room were ramps with completed caskets ready to be boxed.
If you were at the docks, just as I was, the finished products were already boxed and stacked up waiting to be loaded and shipped out.

Over the system, the local radio channel played the song taking me back to the very first time ever being in a big truck. A time when innocents still lived on. Drive by shootings were unheard of. You could walk down the street of Figueroa Blvd during the day or night time without drug dealers and prostitutes on every other corner. And, it was also the first time; I met a number one teenage idol, moms favorite group and got a first real kiss. A moment in time, that will never be forgotten!

It brought a smile to my face, as I began to reminisce back in time to 1972 when I was 8 years old. The most popular car was the VW Beetle. The Vietnam War was still raging but coming to an end. Nixon and the Watergate scandal was all over the news and Apollo 17 landed on the moon. A new TV game show, "The Price Is Right," hosted by Bob Barker was the show to watch. Our thirty third President, Harry Truman and legendary gospel singer Mahalia Jackson both died that year. And on the big screen, the movie, "The Godfather", starring Marlon Brandon grossed $86,691,000. at the box office. It was also the year my oldest brother Will went to fight in the war.

In those years, most of our friends started off in two parent homes and ended up with one parent or grandparent(s) or a guardian watching over them. I had a mom, dad and two big brothers. For me, just being a kid living with my family in a small house on Colden Ave in South Central Los Angeles, California were the best times of my life. Little did I know, life for us would end up in a similar state like our friends.

My parents had a special kind of love that seemed unbreakable. Now don't get me wrong! They weren't George and Louise Jefferson (from the TV sitcom, "The Jefferson's") or Florida and James Evans (the parents of TV sitcom, "Good Times"). There were times when a problem or debate would spark a disagreement but nothing that wouldn't get cleared up by the time we went to bed that night. They'd always kiss, laugh and occasionally dad would bring mom flowers just because. A thing these days a man rarely does without having to be told.

On Saturday's my dad, Greg, was always tinkering around in the garage with older son Will. Will was 18years old at the time and was due to leave with the army that year. Other big brother Bobby, 15 years old, would be out shooting hoops in the driveway. My mom, Nadine, and myself would play albums while cooking and cleaning house. We would sing and dance all over the place as if we were live in concert. Nadine's favorite group was Anita Knight and the Primes. I just loved the Brothers Five. So, both groups music were played a lot.

Nadine had been a nurse for many years but had to stop, when she got sick. She never recovered. Greg never was the same after that. He sold the house and took a job as an over the road truck driver. Bobby and I ended up staying at Aunt Bernice, mother's older sister, house while he worked. She said that when Nadine died, apart of him went with her. The part that made him smile a lot.

It wasn't until later, he decided to take us on a ride with him for the summer. He had hooked up with a company that hauled equipment for some of the pop and r&b groups who would do concert tours. When he wasn't driving it, he'd also assist with the unloading and setting up. It was hard work at times but it kept his mind busy.

His first concert set up that year was in Chicago, IL. I remembered being so excited just to be in another city for the first time. When we arrived, the stage manager gave everyone security passes for the tour. This way if there was any questions as to who belonged back stage it would have an answer by just looking at our tags.

Greg and Bobby got started with the work while I went noising around the arena. It was great watching the workers build the stage and making it come to life with lights and props. The sounds from the house speakers rumbled with music from the instruments on stage. The big red curtains hung to the side of the stage just like window curtains. It was just like watching real life television without the commercials. There were so many rows of seats that it would have taken two hours or more just to count them all.

The band began warming up as I took a seat in the audience to listen. Sitting there, I began to wonder who were the bands set to play on this tour. For some reason, I never thought to ask dad anything like that. Just the excitement of hanging out with him at work was the most important thing in my mind. It was better then going to summer school!

It had been about maybe 5 minutes or so when she walked in. The woman who I spent most of my youth listening to albums and singing in the kitchen with mom. The lady herself, Ms. Anita Knight. As she and the band rehearsed, the first thought was to run and get Greg and

Bobby. But being so memorized, I just couldn't move. The Primes came up shortly after to practice some of those smooth moves and sing just as they always did. There was so much I wanted to tell them about mom and singing their songs while doing housework. But mostly, being Nadine's favorite singer. Listening to her voice sing a verse or two of the songs to be preform that night, my eyes were glued to the stage, watching every move and singing right along with them.

Not long after, another group came into the auditorium. This was such a spectacular surprise because they were my all time favorite group. Five young men, all in my round about age group and were natural brothers from Indiana. They sang, danced and played instruments. It was, "The Brothers Five". They had a string of number one hits that the radio stations labeled, Bubble Gum Music. They were known as the youngest R&B group to come out of the Motor City Sound of the 70ies.

They greeted Ms. Anita by exchanging hugs, before coming down to the audience level to take a seat. And wouldn't you know it, that was right by me. Mr. J, their manager and father, stayed on the stage talking to the stage manager and Ms. Anita. He seemed a little upset about something, but he wasn't getting much attention from the boys or myself.

As, "The Brothers Five" came down to the seating level, I could tell that they were tired and wanted to kick back for a minute or two. They all gave a softly spoken, "Hello", as they took seats around me. Oldest brother of the group, Jack, took the seat right next to me and asked if I was apart of a group preforming on the tour.

Smiling I said, "No, my dad drives the truck for the equipment. He and my brother Bobby were unloading right now."

"A truck driver!" he said with a surprised smile. "Sounds like you are going to be with us the whole tour. What's your name?"

Shaking my head, " Yeah, we are on summer break. My name is Shelby. Shelby Johnson."

"Like the car!" he said shaking my hand.

"That's my dad favorite car," saying proudly. "He said it is a one of a kind model."

Jack smiled delighted by the response. He went on to introduce himself and the rest of the brothers, even though I knew who they were. He was really polite just as they all were. I just couldn't believe, I was having a conversation with one of my all time favorite group. Can't wait to write about this summers adventure when school gets back in!

We didn't get to talk much longer because Mr. J came down to the seating level not as upset as he was earlier on stage with Ms. Anita and the stage manager. He gave them the signal by a head nod and they didn't waste any time moving. He gave this smiling Shelby an unapproved glance as he walked away. My smile soon disappeared at that point briefly.

Standing to his feet, Jack took my hand and kissed it softly saying, "It was a pleasure meeting you Miss. Shelby Johnson. I hope to see you again on the tour," with a wink of an eye.

As he turned to walk away, the smile that once disappeared was now back. It was followed by my blushing face and the soft sounds of giggles from the other brothers, as they departed my company. Then it hit me! I had been so elated with their presents, that I forgot to ask for an autograph. This would had been a tragedy if this was the only time I'd see them. But luckily, this was the beginning of the tour.

Chapter 2

That night before the concert, the stage manager set up a spot for me and Bobby to watch the show in the wings. We sat on some of the stacked equipment cases off to the side in view of the stage. I wore my favorite pink shirt with the flowers and some denim jeans. Hair styled the only way a 10 year old liked best, a pony-tail.

The show was soon to start when Greg and Bobby ended up getting called away to help with stage lights. So just when it looked liked I had a ring side seat to myself, a voice from behind me said, "You mind if I sit here?" Turning surprised, the soft voice was Ms. Anita Knight. Her hair was styled up in a bee hive, wrapped in a scarf and a robe covering her sequence dress of blue with house shoes on her feet. Immediately, I scooted over quickly to give her room to sit down.

She then said, " I always enjoy watching the boys dance. They are so cute."

9

This time, I didn't waste a second asking for her autograph. Ms. Anita asked one of the stage hands to bring over a picture. She signed it, to Shelby with love from Anita Knight! She had heard about me coming along with Greg and Bobby on the truck for the summer tour.

"Maybe we can get together or go shopping if it's alright with your dad," Ms. Anita said with a warm smile. Shaking my head smiling from ear to ear with the delight of her suggestion was my response.

There was a special kinda warm feeling you got just being around her that I found so familiar. Almost like mom sitting right beside me in the kitchen frosting cakes. A thing that was done most every weekend some years ago now. And before you knew it once again, I was off and running in a conversation that lasted through most of, "The Brothers Five" performance. We talked about all the things I wanted to tell her of mom and taking a trip to heaven. Ms. Anita listened and was just as wonderful as her songs.

The conversation ended when she got called away to get ready to go on.

"Thank you for letting me sit with you, Miss Shelby," she said standing up. "We will talk again soon. Hope you enjoy the show."

Being on top of a cloud with an autograph picture was so groovy. I had not yet given any attention to the Brothers

Five until after Ms. Anita was well out of sight. But when I finally looked up, I then realized I had been watched the whole time by Jack and Peter who smiled at me during the performance. The joy of watching a fan sitting and talking with one of their favorite lady of soul singers too must had been a little distracting. Or maybe I was just looking extra pretty in my pink blouse and jeans.

Throughout most of time during the tour, Mr. J kept the brothers pretty busy. Interviews, signing autographs at the local music stores and radio spots in the different cities. It wasn't until the fourth concert stop in Atlanta, Georgia when I got to meet and talked to Peter for the first time. We had waved at each other several times but never a conversation between us. Jack had became friends with Bobby so they played basketball in there spare time a lot by then.

On this day, I was sitting in the front seat of the truck reading one of many storybooks I brought along, when Jack and Peter came by. Jack wanted Bobby to play ball behind the theater on a make shift court some of the guys put together. But he was helping Greg with something in the engine of the truck at the time. Jack hung around anyway to watch and help out. As for Peter, he just wanted to be noisy to see a big truck up close. Greg said it would be alright for me to give him a tour. Made me feel real important!

I showed him the trailer first where all the equipment was stored, then the inside where me, Bobby and dad stayed most of the time. Peter thought it was pretty groovy being on a big truck. He then noticed the books on the dash and wanted to know what I had. I was a real book worm and did a lot of reading for a girl my age. I didn't participate in sports at school or had any interest in the music department. So I guess it's safe to say, I was a Nerd.

I told him of my favorite story, "The Prince and the Pauper." How two boys who looked exactly alike switched lives just by accident. Giving him a small summary of the story, he thought it was a great unbelievable adventure but never read the story for himself. Nothing like his favorite adventure story, Peter Pan. The boy who lived on an island where you never grew up.

Both taking a seat, me at the wheel and him in the jump seat, he then with a smile said, "Anita said you were nice and easy to talk to. Your not at all like a lot of girls we meet. Most of the time, they are always screaming and trying to tear my shirt, even pulling my hair."

Now, to be honest with you, the thought did cross my mine once or twice. This was the lead singer of the group I loved so much! So, in the back of my mind, I thought, "I'd just died and gone to heaven just being in his presents." I was really screaming on the inside.

Trying to sound cool, I just said, "Thanks, your pretty OK yourself," which brought upon the biggest smile on his face.

"So you wanna be friends?" he said.

Before I got the chance to answer, Jack call out for him to come on.

"Sure," I said quickly. "Why don't you hang on to the book for awhile. I can get it back from you later," handing him the book on his way out.

And that's when it happened! He took the book from my hand and lend over to kiss me on the cheek. "Thanks," he said.

Well, after continuously blushing right there in his smiling face, I wanted to just let loose the biggest scream. But contained myself until he was long gone. "I will **NEVER** wash my face again, **EVER!!!!!**"

****

"Excuse me driver," a voice said bringing this truck driver back to the present. It was one of the workers who were loading the trailer. He said the foreman needed me to sign the papers in the office before leaving, which was a normal procedure for transporting loads.

When I got to the office, everyone was engrossed and forced on the television in the waiting area. It was a news alert on CNN. Once the news caster came on, I was even stun by his announcement.

>>>>>>>>>>>>>>>>>>>>>>>

Today, June 25, at 1200pm, 911 received a call that brought an emergency unit to the Westwood, California home of the world legendary king of pop and r&b singer. They found the singer uncontentious and not breathing. He was then rushed to the UCLA Medical Center in Westwood, California where he was pronounced dead due to a Cardioid Dysfunction from a prescription drug overdose, at 1:45 p.m. He was 50yrs.

>>>>>>>>>>>>>>>>>>>>>>>

I couldn't believe what I was hearing. No way! This had to be some kind of a bad joke or Hollywood rumor. And "IT AIN'T FUNNY!" I thought to myself. Pulling out the cell phone to get the truth from the only person who could, it rang only to the incoming call of Bobby. I was slightly disturbed and trying to get him off the phone to make my call when he told me it was true. The statement made me feel numb, shocked and became speechless. I hung up without saying goodbye.

"Here's your paper work," the foreman said. "I have one more box to include as a last minute order. It's already on the shipping papers. The guys are loading it now."

Saying nothing, I signed the papers and went back out to the warehouse. A flood of thoughts and feelings ran through my mind. "What in the world just happen? This can't be! Is it some bad kind of a dream!?"

Chapter 3

It was the last day of the tour and the record label decided to throw a picnic at the beach in Atlantic City, New Jersey. It had been a great tour and a celebration seemed most appropriate. All the artist, stage crew, truck drivers and the band members were in attendance. Dancing to the music on the radio. Bobby and the guys playing football in the sand. Greg at the bar-b-que pit. Mr. J had a domino table going and was he winning, loudly! Peter, Ms. Anita and myself had a card game of, "WAR" going on a blanket under an umbrella on the sand.

"Hey, Anita could you help me out?" one of the other ladies shouted.

"You all keep playing," she said rising to her feet. "I'll be back."

We continued and finished the game. Peter won and made a big deal about it. Whenever he did, it was a major production just like the display his manager Mr. J. was showing. We played cards most of the time of the tour but I won most of the games. Often, we spent time talking about storybooks and home life. We got to be good friends and enjoyed each others company. We had a lot of fun together taking our own tours of the different venues. But now, the tour was over and the fun soon to end.

He said, "We are going to be back in the studio in a couple of weeks laying down tracks for the next album. What about you?"

"Back to school and homework but with the greatest summer story," I said.

Then Peter said something that really changed my out look on celebrities.
"You are the first real friend I ever had that wasn't in the business," he said as his eyes smiled. "Thank you!"

I had never really thought much about what a star goes through until that day. His family had moved all the way from Indiana to California to be closer to the entertainment world. He lost all his friends.

He couldn't go to school or hang out with other kids like I could anymore and he missed that part of his life. All he knew were actors and entertainers like himself. Being a celebrity was not as great as I had imagined it to be. All the money to do whatever you want and can't even go to a fast food place like, Mc Donald's to buy a simple thing as a hamburger without people mobbing you. Can't enjoy an amusement park or just going to the beach without the protection of a body guard. Somebody hiding in the bushes waiting to take your picture for a magazine. Really felt sorry for him!

"I will always be your friend if you want me to be," I said.

Then with a big smile, he reached down in his pants pocket and said,
"I got this for you." He pulled out a beaded bracelet that read:

"We Are Forever"

Reaching for my arm, he put it on. I gave him a big heart felt hug. It was the first nice thing I ever got from a boy. Well, I take that back! I did get the chicken pops from Reggie Henderson in the second grade. Got to stay home for a few weeks and watched TV all day. It was great, no homework! But the scratching wasn't anything nice.

When letting go of our embrace and for the very first time, our eyes met closely. Both blushed this time. There was a long pause of no words between us for that moment. You couldn't hear; the sound of the ocean crashing to the shore, the seagulls over head squalling as they flew by, the music playing and others laughing. It was as if all the sounds of the world left in those few short minutes.

Without a word, Peter leaned over slowly and gave me my first real kiss on the lips. His lips were so soft, just about melted away to the feeling. I had never been kissed by a boy before that day and by a major star was the icing on the cake for a young girl. We closed our eyes embellishing in the sweetness. It had to have lasted at least one full minute without interruption but it felt like the best hour of my life.

****

"KABOOOOM!!!!" was the sound that came from the back of the trailer.

"Oh no, not that!" I mumbled while pulling over to the shoulder of the highway.

Getting out to check what I had already suspected, one of the inside dual tires had blown out on the trailer. If I were to call it in, it would take a roadside service at least 3 to 4 hours to get out there to replace it. So instead, very cautiously, I drove on it about 10 or 15 miles to the next truck stop to get it fix. At least this way, I could be close to a bathroom and food if it takes to long.

The Waffle House with a truck shop right next door call, "Al's Auto Shop," was where I ended up. They had an area for big trucks to park over night and a shower set up inside. The mechanic said he could replace the tire but he didn't have one that size at his shop. He would have to go into town 20 miles away to a tire vendor to get one. It was going to be a few hours before the big white truck could get rolling again.

"Might as well do my 10hrs shut down here and pick it up later tonight," I thought walking toward the diner.

Once inside, I found a very homely type of atmosphere. It had about 3 booths and 4 tables with chairs and a small bar counter for those who wanted to eat alone. There were two waitress' taking orders and a cook in the back. If you sat at the counter you could watch him cook. I took a seat at a booth and one of the waitress', Carol, came over to take my order.

The television mounted on the far wall, was on. Wouldn't you know it, it was CNN talking about the tragedy again. Most of the people in the diner were watching and talking amongst themselves about the broadcast. But as for me, glued to it would be more accurate. I wanted to hear it again and get more detail on what happened.

The singer had never been that badly sick and appeared pretty healthy from what all had seen in his performances, so said the news report. The topic this time was about the doctor. They were discussing how he made the call and left the scene. How his licenses was suspended and what his part was in this tragic death. So why is a healthy man dead? The more I listened, the madder I could feel myself getting. Carol came over to the table with a glass of water and the menu.

"Sorry 'bout that," she said with a southern drawl in her voice. "I've been so in shock about what happen. He was one of my most favorite singers."

"It's okay," I respond. "He was my favorite too."

"Just to think, how dumb was this doctor," she went on to say. "Not to have anything ready in case of an emergency. I hope he goes to jail, cause if it was left up to me, his butt would be under the jail."

"Yeah, your right," agreeing with a slight laughter at her conclusion of sentencing.

As she took the order, it wasn't long for us to engage chatting like old high school friends. I told her about the truck tire and needing to get to California for delivery. Carol assured me that Al's shop were kinda slow but does a good job on truck repair. She even offered shower privileges just in case I wanted to relax for a while. A grateful offer.

After Carol brought the order, I invited her to sit since it was slow in the diner. She was due for her break anyway so it was timed just right. Carol went on to tell me of how she met her husband at her prom. They danced their first dance to, "You Are The Lady Of My Life". Apparently, she went with another guy to the prom who got drunk and passed out in the parking lot before they even got inside. And that's when her husband stepped in. He came stag. He put the guy in the car to sleep it off and took her inside to the prom. He was her knight in shinning armor.

She married him later and danced to the same song at there reception. Her story was so sweet and romantic. But now after 10yrs the man who sung there love Ballard was gone. The hurt was felt in her voice as well as inside my heart little did Carol know. She would never know how much. I had a secret friendship and there it would stay. It was "NOT" for the world to share in under any terms even now.

We talked about the first time, "Thriller" came on MTV, the movie "The Wiz," and how the "Moonwalk" at the Motown 25yr reunion was the most exciting thing ever seen. It was nice socializing with a real fan. One of many fans I would come across on this trip to California. When Carol returned to her duties and while there, I tried to get thru to the main house to get some real answers, other than what was on the news. But the signal for the cell phone was so poor, that every try was cut off again and again. "Dam, Should have gotten Verizon"!

At least, 4hours had gone by before one of the shop guys came in to let me know the job was finish. Being tired from waiting, I decided to go ahead with the first thought and shut down 10hrs there. This way, when I started back up to drive, I'd have a full 11 hours on the log book to drive without a penalty. A truck drivers regulated law that is enforced by DOT.

I had a sleeper style truck so a bed was always ready an available at any time. Paying the bill on the way out, I thanked Carol for her company and service by handing her a tip. I felt like now, whenever I came back through, there was a friend. Handing a napkin to me, she said, "If you would, could you put this on his star for me?" I opened it and there was a silver cross with an inscription:

"To God Be The Glory"

It left me a little speechless. Here it was a stranger who never really knew him on a personal level wanted to pay her respects by sending a gift.

"Sure, I will," I said.

This was one of the first gestures on the trip back that was being sent with heart felt love and condolences to a man they never got to meet. But funny how it was given to one who loved him as well. I placed the napkin in my pocket for safe keeping.

As I walked back to the truck, thoughts of all the love from fans that stretched out all across the world began flooding my mind. There wasn't anybody on the planet that didn't here of him or know his work. He had grown to be a household name. Who knows, they may have even heard of him out there in the galaxy as well. The invincible Capt. E.O. But now because of a flat tire, I got to feel people who were touched by his music in sweet wonderful ways. Music that generations will still be singing songs and doing those same unbelievable moves for years to come. I felt proud of being apart of it.

Chapter 4

From time to time, Peter and I got to hang out with each other between school and tours. Sometime for a few hours, others for the whole day. Most of the time, we talked on the phone for hours until someone told us to get off cause they wanted to use the phone.

We had gone to the beach and Disneyland more times than anybody could remember and that's where the name Minnie came in. He kept getting taller every time we went but I didn't grow as fast. He teased me about it and started calling me, Minnie. One would think now just because Mickey was Minnie's counter partner, he would get that nickname. I just called him Peter.

It got to the point that when we called each other over the phone, we'd ask for each other by those names. "Hello, is Minnie there?", he would say. Or, "May I speak to Peter?" is what I would say. Both families even called those names out loud to us. And like most things that are

25

enjoyable in our lives, the names stuck through teenage years, even into adult life.

One evening when I was about 15years old, I had planned to spend time at home watching the I Love Lucy Marathon with Aunt B. and dad. Peter came over before it started with the biggest surprise. He had heard that the school had a dance going on that night at the Disneyland Hotel but I didn't plan on going. Peter wanted to go.

"I can't go to no dance," I said standing there in the living room with my hair tied up in a ponytail, pajamas and house shoes.

He just gave that very sincere smile, "Don't worry I got it covered just come on with me".

"What about Aunt B. and dad?" I said. "They were looking forward to…"
And at that moment, Greg came in the room dressed in his work cloths caring a duffel bag.

"Sorry baby girl, I got to go. Your Aunt B went to bed, said maybe next time. A driver had an emergency and can't take a load out to Arizona," he said kissing my cheek as he started out the door. "See you kids later, and have a good time at the dance," while closing the door on his way out.

"Well I guess that settles that," Peter said holding out his gloved covered hand to receive mine. "Let's go!" Grabbing my hand and out the door we went to the waiting limo out front.

The first stop was on Rodeo Drive to the cloths stores. It didn't take long to find a very nice party dress with shoes to match! He had already saw the dress and thought it would look great on me. Red silk with ruffle short sleeves, v-neck cut, straight length to the knee.

The next stop was a hair salon two doors over. The stylist had been alerted by Peter days ago. It took a little while but she gave me the latest hair style. A Farrah Fawcett looking, "Page-Boy." You could tell by the look on Peter's face, it met to his approval. Now, I was really ready for the dance. So once again, off in the limo we went to the event.

While at the cloths store, I had picked up something for Peter. I knew how he always wore gloves all the time to cover the discoloration on his hands due to the on going skin problem. He'd been hiding it from the public for years with body make up, long sleeves and gloves.

"I thought you might like this," handing him a single white glove with diamond studded rhinestones covering the top side of it.

"This is cool! I love it! Thank you Minnie!" he said.

He put it on and began doing hand motions like a mime. It came to life just by being on his hand. He wore it all the time since that night for many years. The one glove became a trademark on one of his albums. It even made it to the tabloids and he wore it proudly. Wouldn't you know it was just like him turn it into a fashion statement. Can't give him anything!

Once we arrived at the hotel ballroom, the dance was already in full swing. We were both at "Ahh" of all the decorations. They made it up to look like Cinderella and Prince Charming's Castle. Beautifully soft lite chandler and strobe lights lite up the room. Along with a live band, big dance floor, the works, it was great. Mickey and Minnie were even in attendance dressed for the party and dancing. It had all the makings of a fantasy night out.

Playing at the time was a slow love song. Peter took me straight out to the center of the floor into the crowd of already dancing people right next to Mickey and Minnie for the first dance of the evening. He held me close and tight in his arms. Our bodies felt like one swaying back and forth to the music. I laid my head on his chest with closed eyes drowning myself in the moment. "He smelled so nice!" I thought.

Softly in my ear, he began to sing the words to the song. It was all so romantic. Both knew that once he was spotted, it wouldn't be as magical as it was at that moment.

"I'm glad you made me go to this....." pausing and looking up to him in wonderment. "Wait, how did you know about the dance anyway? I didn't say anything about a dance."

"Shh, this is the best part of the song," pulling me close again to avoid an answer. "♪♪..Love in your own special way, ♪..love all my heart away, with a smile...♪♪"

It made me smile to see he was having so much fun dancing with me. But then, the Assist. Principal stopped the band to make an announcement. She had heard that Peter was there and invited him up to the stage to preform with the band. The room went wild with cheers and applauds. He didn't want to leave me but I gave him the okay to go do what he does so well. Kissing my cheek with a smile and a wink, away he went and the magic between us was over.

Once on stage, he greeted the band and gave the Assist. Principal a big hug. Even she was a big fan and swoon in his arms. Taking the mic, he began to sing one of his songs right away and it got everyone going. I moved closer to the side of the stage set up just to watch him preform just as I did the first time I watched him preform years ago with his brothers. He was still just as mystifying and dynamic as ever even without, "The Brothers Five" being by his side doing slick moves.

Later on the way home, he told the story of when he called the house. Bobby told him about the dance. Dad had been trying to get him to take me. That wasn't going to happen! Who wants to be seen in public by friends taking their kid sister out any where. Bobby was the big time ball player, most popular guy on campus. I wasn't and didn't have the for thought of being out there like that. Dad thought it would be a great idea to get me out the house for a change. That's when Peter decided to skip out on an award ceremony Mr. J had scheduled for him. The dance would be over early so we wouldn't get caught. And we didn't. Wow, what a break!

Chapter 5

Who would have thought after 4yrs at U.C.L.A in Westwood California for a R.N degree in nursing, Shelby Johnson would end up driving a big truck? And wouldn't you know it, best friend Peter went to college with me too. But that's a story you'll read in another chapter.

My immediate family, always knew that one of the boys would be the one to take over whatever ground work dad laid out. And I was to follow in moms foot steps in the nursing field. My dad, Greg, worked as the local trashman for more then 15yrs before even thinking about the trucking business. In his youth, he had saved up enough money to open his own garage. The old shop over on Broadway and Century was owned by Mr. Hill and he was retiring from the business. They had an agreement if Greg came up with at least half of what he was asking for he'd turn it over to him.

One Friday night, the community center in the neighborhood was giving a dance. My mom, Nadine, was there on a date with her girlfriend brother that worked at the same company with Greg. The guy was clearly not her type and watching from across the room Greg knew it. So when the opportunity came, he went up to her and introduced himself. Now you can say what you want, but Nadine always said, it was love at first sight. A thing that's not around as much.

Now, Nadine was already in school getting her nursing degree at the time. But soon after they started dating, she got pregnant. Greg did the noble thing and married her. Boy, was Gran-Mommy mad. Greg insisted on her finishing school and she did. Nadine got her degree as an LVN and a job soon followed. Greg encouraged and did everything he could to make her happy. She always knew his plans with buying the shop so they always kept a small savings to try and make that dream come true. He never did get that shop.

They went on to have three children. Greg taught the boys about small engines and hard work. The oldest, Will, worked closely with him. They would spend most of there Saturday's, tinkering around on lawn mowers and the old car we had. Will wanted to open a shop for him and dad one day. He wanted to fulfill dad's dream, since he could not for raising us. But he never got the chance, after going into the armed forces.

Bobby, on the other hand, wanted to play basketball. So every chance he got, he was in the driveway shooting hoops with some of the guys on the block. He went on to play in high school but not in college. Then one day, he came home from school and didn't want to play it any more. He took down all his posters, put the ball in a box and took it to the garage. I can't recall ever knowing why! But he would later end up driving a truck with dad for a few years until he decided to become a business manager.

My mom, Nadine, had been a nurse for several years at Buckingham Memorial Hospital until I was 8yrs. She was the assistant staff manager over her floor and still did the required nursing duties. I would go with her on occasions to work just to see what she did. I thought it was great to help other people try to get back what they lost due to an accident or some kind of physical handicap brought on by a sickness or injury. Nadine had a warm caring touch for the job and everyone loved her. I wanted to be just like her.

But the year she caught a cold and couldn't shake it, was when she had to stop working. The doctor said that she needed to take a break from work because she wasn't letting herself fight the infection off with the proper rest. We all pitched in to make her job a little easier around the house, but she just wasn't getting any better. She knew that her time was coming to an end but did not want us to worry.

Every evening before going to bed, I would crawl into bed with her and read stories like, "The Prince and the Pauper." But this one night, Nadine wanted to tell me another story, about a little girl taking a boat ride down the river. It was a beautiful story. Later, I realize this story was about her and the journey, she was about to go on without us.

The cold turned into pneumonia and on April 16th, she passed away at home with me, Bobby and Greg. Will was away in the army at the time, but he came home for the funeral. He was never seen again after that. Four months later, Greg received a letter from the army stating Will was missing in action. Thinking back on it today, we never saw dad cry throughout any of it. Not even at the funeral. He just stopped!

Aunt B, Bernice, Nadine's oldest sister, loved us and children very much. She had no children of her own so we had often visited her on the west side of town, 107th and Figueroa Blvd. Bernice suggested that we stay with her until Greg was able to get himself together. Her husband killed himself long before I was born. They say, he lost his job and went to the store one night to get some beer. The next day, they found him in his car on the parking lot of the store dead due to a self inflicted gunshot wound to the head. The beer was still in the bag unopened.

Greg left the trash company and started driving trucks. It gave him a chance to be alone to work out his thoughts and feelings. After a while, Greg really got into the trucking thing. It seemed as if he was finding his way back from all the turmoil that overcame him. He still didn't smile that much, but he was some what better. Greg later put together a company of his own with 25 trucks and a shop.

Bobby was due to graduate in a few years after that summer we went with dad on the tour but no idea as to what he was going to do. As stated before, it was all about the round ball on the court. That's when dad started grooming him for trucking. He did drive for a few years until he decided on college.

Your thinking, now this must be about the time I got into truck driving don't you? Nope, that didn't come about til way much later after college. Keep reading!

Chapter 6

Jack, being the oldest and the only one in, "The Brothers Five" with a drivers license, would often bring Peter over to hang out. He and Bobby had stayed pretty close friends. Basketball buddies is best described. It was always some game going on in the backyard. But Aunt B just thought, they just loved the cookies she baked. That was the first thing they would ask about when they came through the front door. She always had a bunch cooking when she knew they were coming.

Sometime, the boys would play all day. I wasn't that good at it but Jack would always encourage me to play at least one game. Me and Jack against Peter and Bobby. The fun, the laughter, the loud conversations, priceless! Those were the years when needing a bodyguard wasn't necessary if you dressed a certain way. Like you belonged in the neighborhood. But Mr. J, their dad and manager, was very protective of the boys and didn't like the idea of them coming down to that part of town. He felt they had no need to relive the Indiana days. So when they could get away for a few hours, the Johnson's house would get a visit. Visits were always filled with fun.

This went on for awhile, until that day Mr. J found out where they really were. It was a Sunday afternoon. Jack and Bobby were playing one on one. Greg had just got in off the road and was taking a shower. Aunt B was napping on the couch in the front room. Peter and I were in Auntie's old 1968 Cadillac parked in front of the house pretending, to be off on another adventure. Peter was behind the wheel.

"You know, you really should learn how to drive," I tease.

"I know how to drive, Minnie", he'd say.

"Oh yeah, I think your making that up. I can even drive now."

"I can too," he said. "If we had keys, I would take you around the block and prove it to you."

"And what the hell are you doing in this car?" a voice said standing by the window on the driver side. It was Mr. J and was he mad. "Get out the car. Now! Where is Jack?" he asked.

Just then as he was questioning us, the ball came rolling out of the backyard down the drive with Jack chasing it.

Once he saw Mr. J, the signs of fun ended on his face. All the laughter he and Bobby made playing basketball was now just an echo of the fun for the day. He knew, they were in big trouble by just seeing the tall stocky built man.

Mr. J began to fuss at them for being gone so long that nobody knew where they were. The anger in his voice scared me too. I never heard our dad get that mad and we did a lot of dumb stuff too. Bobby came out to see what was taking so long for Jack to return with the ball only to catch the scolding of Mr. J.

The joy of a beautiful sunny day had ended. The boys were given orders to get in the car to leave at once. Mr. J gave that same unapproved look to us just as he gave me back on the tour. I had never even told dad about the look he'd given me now more then once. Bobby and I said not a word. I just chucked it up as, just the way he looked. They waved good bye as Mr. J drove off with Jack and Peter in one car and the chauffeur following in the other car.

By the time Greg came out to see why it was so quiet, they were gone. Bobby and I just sat there on the porch. We told him, what happened and he explained why Mr. J was so mad. He wanted to make sure they were safe at all times. Yes, they were still kids like we were but their lives were changing. They couldn't go back to the way it used to be in Indiana. The world wasn't going to let them. Guess, you never think about the fact of someone doing harsh

things to your friends by just coming over for cookies and
basketball on a Sunday.

****

"Swoosh....Pssss!" went the sound as the parking brake was
released the at the rest area. It had been some miles. I needed
a stretch break. Most of the rest areas came equipped with
restrooms,vending machines and picnic areas. A good place
to relax for a few minutes before continuing the drive.

As I was doing a standard walk around pretrip check
on the rig, a bus pulled in with what looked like steam
coming out of the rear. It parked next to me and everyone
started getting out heading toward the restrooms. Some
talking about the bus overheating and wondering if they
were going to make it in time to California.

The driver, who was also a woman, came over to ask
about a water container. As a truck driver, it is always a
necessity having extra fluids while on the road. You never
know when you were gonna need it. Bus' don't always have
the space for these things. They usually make enough stops
to be at a place where any repairs can be made in a hurry
to continue down the road. But every once in a while, they
do run into problems like this.

I loaned her the water container and assisted with the
task. But just as we were finishing up on pouring coolant
in the radiator in the distance, the sound of an ambulance
could be heard coming in our general direction. Never did

I think, it was coming into the rest area. When it arrived, they stopped right in front of the bus and across from the restrooms. Two EMS workers got out and hurried toward the building pulling a gurney.

Soon after, they were bringing a lady out on the gurney. The driver remembered her from being on the bus, so we both hurried over to the EMS truck. Another lady with her was standing by as the driver talked to the woman and the EMS. Apparently, she had not taken her medicine and passed out. They had her on oxygen while she laid back on the stretcher.

The woman looked to be in her late forties. Apparently, she was on several different blood pressure medicines but did not take them on time for a couple of days. They had to take her to the nearest medical center right away. She could not complete the journey to California as she had hoped, neither could her companion. The driver spoke to both of the ladies before moving away from the vehicle letting them know where there luggage would end up.

Then just as they were about to close the rear doors of the van to take the woman on the gurney away, she reached out to grab my hand giving an envelope. She spoke breathlessly through the oxygen mask.

"Take this the rest of the way for me," she said. Then the doors closed and the van was on its way.

It wasn't until they were out of site and the others went back to the bus when I looked at the envelope. It read: An Icon. Opening it with the driver in attendance, inside was an old picture of a little girl about 4 or 5years old, who appeared to be a burn patient. The driver said she spoke of her daughter several times on the trip and that the child died a few years ago. We came to the conclusion, that this must had been her child. She was taking the trip to California to put it with all the memorabilia gathered at the Hollywood Star.

Once again, I was entrusted to take another special gift on this ride. But this time, an even more heart felt one. You see, I remembered the child in the picture because I took the picture many years ago. Her name was Keri. One of the children at the hospital, where I worked as a nurse. She had the biggest smile a child could give and was wrapped in the arms of Peter sitting on her hospital bed. It nearly brought a tear to my eye just looking at their faces. Both gone to soon!

Chapter 7

By senior year of high school, Jack had gotten married and started a family of his own. Peter on the other hand, had his own personal driver and bodyguard. A guy by the name of Gerald. He was 6'2ft and weighed about 250lbs of nothing but muscle. He was BIG!

Visits were sometime a little weird having someone watching over you as we played cards. Very distracting! But this Saturday, Gerald wanted to watch the game with Bobby on cable. He had been at the house several times so he was treated just like everybody else. Aunt B left to go shopping and wouldn't be back for awhile. Dad hadn't got back yet off the road, so it was just the kids home for the day.

In the kitchen making sandwiches, Peter brought up the subject he and I had on that day in the car when Mr. J came to the house. He recalled the conversation.

"Remember I told you, I could drive?" he said reaching in the cabinet over the sink for the potato chips.

"Yeah," I said smiling never looking up from spreading mayo on the bread. "But I knew you couldn't really."

"Well, how about I take you on that ride around the block today?"

"Get out! You still can't drive. You got other people to do that for you."

After putting down the bag of chips, he pulled out a set of car keys from his pocket. "Let's go for a ride," he said with a grin dangling the keys in front of my face.

He had a set of car keys made for himself in the event, there was an urgency to get in while he and Gerald were out in public. And since Gerald was so involved with Bobby and the game that day, he set it up so we could get away for an hour or two alone. If there was any time in our entire life we would look back on as, the worse thing best thing, this would be it. Clearly this was going to be a huge mistake. We were teens and that's what we do!

Finishing up on all the sandwiches and putting them in a big cooler, Peter took some of them in to Bobby and Gerald. He made up some excuse about playing cards til a thousand points and went back in the kitchen. He gave Bobby the, "Hi-sign", and the next thing I knew, we were driving away unnoticed.

He drove around the neighborhood at first. Then we went to see the Watts Towers, the Goodyear tire mountains on Alameda Blvd and drove through Huntington Park to see the shops. I had seen all these places many times before but never with my best friend in the car. It was exciting! So exciting that when we stopped at a light on Pacific Blvd in Huntington Park, who do you think was crossing the street right in front of us carrying shopping bags? Yep, Aunt B. We panic and then ducted down trying to go unnoticed. If she'd caught us, the ride would be over right then and there. But she didn't and we left that part of town in a hurry.

"Minnie, you remember the story you gave me once about the Prince and the Pauper?" Peter said.

"What about It?"

Hesitating he said, "I think, I could pull that off."

"It's just a kids story, that's all."

"I know but just hear me out. See, I got to thinking of how he made his escape to freedom by changing lives with the other kid," he went on to say.
"I could do the same thing too."

"The other kid in the story was his exact double," I reminded him. "So what, you wanna try and clone yourself or something?"

Pulling over and stopping, "Listen, my looks are starting to change now and more and more people are out there dressing like me everyday. Some even look like me a little. The plastic surgeries aren't so bad any more. I could escape this side of the world forever if I wanted to and no one would even know it."

"But you love the stage, the lights and the applauds," I said. "You want to give it all up now?"

"Yeah, I do love the stage an all but one day, I want to grow old in a nice little home with someone. Without the paparazzi looking in the window all the time," he said. "I want to have kids and they don't live through the nightmare I had to live in the public eye all the time."

"Look, even if you did do this transforming thing with somebody, your family would still know it's not you," I said. "Besides, some of us true fans would know it's not you if the other person starts to sing."

"Didn't think about that part." Snaps his fingers, "He can use sound tracks! I'm telling you this could work."

"So what are you saying?" I said with a slight attitude. "You want out of the business? Out of the life you've known all these years to do what? Go back to Indiana, away from all of us?"

He gets out the car to come opens my door and kneels down, "Look, all I'm saying is, if one day a man comes up to you, takes you by the hand and say something like, ONLY YOU, WOULD EVER KNOW THE SUCCESS OF TRUE FREEDOM. He's just letting you what he found," he said with a calm voice.

I was bewildered by what he meant by just telling me all that, until college. In those years, he came in several different disguises.
But even then, he didn't do or say the same words he spoke today. He always let me know it was him. Nothing about succeeding to escape or leaving the business this way. When I got out the car, the subject was soon dropped. It didn't come back up throughout the rest of our time together that day. But the thought still lived in the back of my mind for sometime.

The ride ventured us up to my school. There, we had a picnic lunch out front on the stone steps of George Washington High. It was turning out to be the best day, until a 1964 blue Chevy low-rider pulled up to the curve. It was the car of one of the local gang members, 8-ball. He had three of his homeboys along with him. Baby Rock, Dirt and Slim. All well known hoodlums around the neighborhood and school.

"Wha' dup cuz?" 8-ball said getting out of the car with the others following.

"Hey, look ya'll, they got lunch for us."

"Let's go," I said starting to get up.

"No," Peter said holding my arm. "If we run, they will chase right after us."

I wasn't afraid for myself, much. But if they figured out who he was, it could become a nightmare. Peter was real cool about the whole thing. They were dressed in their gang colors of blue. Rags hung out of their back pocket jeans that sagged below there waist line. 8-ball carried a gun and it could be seen under his shirt slightly.

What started out as a potential harassment went well after Slim identify Peter. Peter had became so popular by then that the hard heads turned like little girl fans. They were so excited! They loved his music and style. Took me for a loop! Big bad killers going wild over a star. This was history in the making.

They laughed together and exchange hip hop mouth Beat Box beats. They showed Peter dance moves like, "The Crip Walk." Did "Raps" that were in fact pretty good. Peter even taught them some of his slick moves. It was just an amazing thing to watch an artist at work.
He had more fun with them, then they did with him. He took their numbers and told them he was thinking of doing a gang scene video and wanted to use them. Local

kids in a video, was like having a dream come true if you were from the hood like them.

It had started to get late and we had to get back in a hurry. I knew the fastest way to get home so I navigated once we were back in the car. The game would be over soon and getting caught was not apart of the adventure trip list for the day. When we reached the block, Aunt B had just got there also and was headed up to the door with bags in her arms, not seeing us. We crept slowly down the street to put the car back in place like it was when we left.

"Slow down. If she sees us........." I said to Peter who was driving.

"......I can't!" he said mashing on the brake frantically. "It won't stop!"

"Do something! You gonna hit Aunt B," I said in a panic. **"Oh, my goodness!"**

The brakes had been acting a little funny most of the ride. Now, they were gone and the car was on a rolling pathway toward Aunt B. Peter began blowing the horn as I yelled out to get her attention to move. Once she saw what was coming at her, she got out the way just in time. We hit the trashcans and crashed landed in the rose bushes in the front yard to stop. It made such a noise it brought Bobby, Gerald and Greg, who was now home, out to the front porch. The looks on those faces could never be described.

"BUSTED!!!"

Chapter 8

Some days the trucking business can really be a pain when the weather change up on you. This is why it is important that drivers always keep to the rules of following distance in mind at all times. People who don't drive professionally, don't get this even though this is the first thing they learn before they receive their drivers license. It's forgotten and lost in there memory, until an accident occurs. I had seen some bad accidents out there on the road over the few years I've been a driver.

It's still warm out and raining cats and dogs. The Summer Storm passing through Arkansas slowed traffic down to at least 40 mph. The 8 second eye lead rule was now up to 10 seconds. The windshield wipers weren't moving fast enough to see and the need of a restroom asap had now started to become an issue. Then suddenly the cars in front of me, hit there brakes and brought all the traffic to a stop. I turned up the CB to hear what was going on. Maybe the road flooded out.

"Got a brake check at mile marker 196," one guy said.

"Whats going on with the brake check?" I asked.

"Got a 10-33 on the west bound side. Greyhound bus rear ended a emergency vehicle in the median," he said. "Gonna be there for a minute, no lanes open."

I was to far back to see anything other then red tail lights. The wall of rain made it even harder to see. I knew, I was close to that stretch of highway by at least 5 miles or so. Other drivers were on the CB talking about what they saw and giving there analysis of the accident like they always do. So after about 10 minutes and no one moving, I released the brake and jumped in the back bunk section of the cab to find a cup and napkins to use it. Just couldn't hold it any more.

****

It was a Thursday night when a limo driver knocked at the door of my Aunt's house to pick me up. I was ready in a navy blue evening gown, hair all dazzled up with my most fearest high heel shoes and a small glitter purse with matching earrings and bracelet. I was on point! The driver escorted me to the car and opened the door. Peter stepped out with the biggest smile looking very handsome in a black tuxedo. White shirt, bow tie, the works!

"You look, fabulous," with his eyes ready to jump out his head.

"You looking pretty sharp yourself mister, But could you have worn different shoes for a change?" pointing to his feet to a pair of hush puppies he always wore.

"I like these shoes. They're comfortable," he said. "What!?"

"Forget it," shaking my head and getting in the car.

Inside the limo were two other starlet friends of his who names can't be revealed at this time. But I can tell you this, one was a top well known model back in the 80's and the other a motion picture star they said he was dating. They were beautiful and me too. I was now a young 20 year old adult and didn't mind dressing up more. This is my first night out in his world to the premier of his first major movie at the Chinese Theater in Hollywood.

The closer we got to the theater, the more nervous I had gotten. The girls were great. They assured me, it would be fine and tried there best to ease my fears. It wasn't working! I had never gone with him to such an event. I didn't live in his world of glamor and cameras. So far, the public world had not seen us any where together, only the kids from school now some years back. Our secret lives was about to be out in the open. A thing, I did and didn't want to be apart of by just watching what Peter went through all those years.

The limos line up on the boulevard. One by one, they pulled up on cue for the celebs to get out for the cameras at the red carpet. When our limo got to the carpet, I squeezed his hand even tighter. The door opened and the girls got out first. The crowd and cameras were going wild. Peter shut the door and instructed the driver to go leaving the other two on the carpet. We circled the block and pulled into the lot of other limos and stop.

To the driver, "Could you excuse us for a minute please," Peter said.

The driver looking in his rear view mirror said not a word. With a nod of his head, turned off the car and got out as requested. Then Peter looked into my eyes just as he did the day on the beach. He smiled and spoke very softly.

"I'm sorry! Minnie, you have been my best-friend now for a long time. All I wanted to do was share this moment with you just like you've shared great times with me," holding both my hands. "You mean so much to me. But if your uncomfortable about this, we can go back to the house, pig out on pizza and watch movies. Just say the word," he said with a seriousness about himself.

"You'd miss your own premier for me? I can't let you do that. This is your big night," I said. "I just feel like... I

53

would be messing it up for you. I'm a not a star or a model. I'm a nobody."

Raising his voice slightly, "Not to me! Minnie...." Singing the next few words, " ♪..Your love is magical, ♪..that's how I feel..♪♪..But in your presence, ♪..I am lost for words.♪♪ ..words ♪♪..like. Shelby, I...I love you."

The fear I felt was now at ease. With a now calming smile, all I could and wanted to say all these years was simple, "I always..... loved you."

I guess it comes to a point when you just can't dance around what you feel when you care so much for someone. With so much love, passion and all the feelings we had for each other inside, it just went rushing right through our bodies when we embraced. Every woman in the world wanted to be in that same exact spot at that moment. I was living it for all of them.

What happened next was just like something written right out of a romance novel but not as elaborate. He touched me in a place so deep it sent chills down my spine. The heat of his body coming out of his shirt made me even hotter. Didn't even care about a hair-do at this point. It wasn't the first time nor the last time I ever made out in the back seat of a car. The only thing different was, this car had plenty of back seat to work with.

****

"Honk, Honk, Honk, Honk!" The cars behind the big truck started to blow.

The rain storm had passed and the road opened up for one lane to get through. The traffic in the rear view mirror was as far back as the eye could see. Voices over the CB were still talking about the pile up. And the horns brought me back from the past just a little bit to soon from an enjoyable encounter.

As I got closer to where the accident had occurred, it was nothing left to see. The ambulance was on the back of a tow truck smashed to bits. The Greyhound Bus was empty and being hauled out of the ditch. It had a major dent in the side. Surely, there were casualties. Increasing your following distance whether you are in a car, bus or truck should always be a thing in mind all the time. Nothing is more important then that!

Oh yeah, about that night of the premier, I did walk the red carpet that night with him and smile. The cameras were gone inside and no one saw us slip by. We were fashionably late!

Chapter 9

The smell of nature and beauty of the countryside are daily joys. The loads hauled were mostly drop n hook and occasionally I help to unload. This load was going directly to Forest Lawn Mortuary in California where workers unloaded. It had a schedule appointment. The slow downs of the tire and rain had not become a problem at this time.

As I pulled into the Amarillo, TX. Flying J truck stop for fuel and a bathroom break, a crowd lingering in the parking lot in front of the station could be seen. The Rigs parking area had a few people wondering around shooting pictures. First thought was, these were tourist and like always they are fascinated with the different designs, colors and fashions of the trucks on display. Nothing I haven't seen before over the years.

Over the CB, some of the drivers were talking about the crowd and them being tourist. Come to find out, they were all fans going by the bus loads to California to pay there last respects. Wow, it had to be at least 100 or more people out there at the time in 90 degree dry heat. They were all on a break. What a turn out to see!

After pumping fuel, I parked the truck and did my log book before going over. I had gone well over a thousand miles on this trip already. There was time so no need to eat and run like I did most times. Besides, I wanted to get a close up look at the mass of people that were making the journey before going in.

As I walked amongst them, there were people of all races, ages and genders grouped off or coupled off talking and laughing. Some girls were singing his songs aloud and enjoying the moment of being like him. Some wore t-shirts with his picture on them in several well known poses. A couple of guys had on the famous red and black jackets from the gang video he did make with 8-Ball and his crew of misfits. These were everyday folks who took time away from there lives to go on a quest to honor a legend in the world of music. It still felt like a bad dream.

****

When I moved out to college, Peter had become a solo artist and wrote most of his music. He was doing a lot of promoting all over the world. From time to time, he did guest spots with the Brothers Five but the group just took a back seat to his now evolving career.

His songs were reaching record highest in 12 different countries by then. It became harder and harder for him to maintain his privacy. When he went out with known celebrity starlets, it was like breaking news. The cameras were always watching his every move. He got no peace of his own unless he was behind the gates of the Havenhurst house where his family resided.

I didn't hear from him that much the first year. As a matter of fact, I only recalled just talking to him once over the phone about 2am right around spring mid terms. I had been studying a lot and didn't come back to the room til late when the library closed. Sleep would be the only thing I was looking forward to when going back to the room. But one night he called and sleep became the last thing I would get.

"Ring, ring, ring, ring...." I answered the phone still sleep one eye open to check the time. "Hello, this better be good."

"Hey Minnie!" the voice on the other end said. "How's school coming?"

After recognizing just who it was, I immediately began to wake up. "Peter! Where are you?" I said turning on the light, "You know what time it is?"

He gave a slight laugh and apologize for the time difference. He was in Tokyo doing a performance and wanted to know if I got the record he sent.

"Yeah, I got it," saying while reaching over to the side of the bed to pick it up. "Got a good beat to it and all, but I can't understand a word of it. It's in Japaneses!"

Again he gives a slight laugh, "I'm sorry. Promise, I'll send you another in English, okay?"

We both laughed about the mistake. It was good to hear his voice and there was so many things I wanted to ask him about his excursions around the world. He had a way of painting some of the most exciting pictures in my mind of where he was. And at 2am 8hrs away from the last exam, I didn't mind a nice picture to go back to sleep on. But for some reason, tonight was different. There was something else in his voice. Never would I ask, what was troubling him. Usually, I just let him talk until he's ready to say. And he did!

"Shelby," he said, a name he most never called out loud. "This thing on my hand is getting harder to cover up. It's starting to spread all over." Sadly he went on, "I'm afraid everyone is gonna find out and laugh at me and call me a freak."

I paused for a moment. This is my best friend and I just couldn't stand to hear him sound so hurt. He had been faced with this challenge since he was a kid. Trying to cover up the blotches with body make up before a public appearance and now it was starting to take on an ugly effect to his eyes and mind.

Being Shelby, I simply said, "You no what? F**k 'em! Tell them, if they don't like it, to just kiss your A***! If they got a problem with that, I'll get some big guys and we can just throw down on them."

With my being apart of the outside life of stardom, it gave him another escape avenue. Those few vulgar words, that he never says out loud, brought him back to the laughter we always shared. I understood what he was feeling more so then anybody else. I wasn't as pretty as most of the girls he knew so being looked at as ugly was not unfamiliar to me. Besides, if I didn't make him laugh right away, he would make me cry.

The conversation that night went on til dawn, ranging from the serious side of life, to the funniest things of all time.
We talked about one day having kids and what type of world they would live in. The challenges of being famous vs being common folks. He always felt that my outlook was a honest way of him feeling some what normal, a thing he could be only in a day dream. Peter needed that freedom for a while considering his fear.

The Vitiligo was taking over and getting worse. The body make up, gloves, long sleeves, long pants, were beginning to not be enough coverage to the on going problem. There wasn't any cure any where in the world. It changed his skin color to a lighter shade of brown. He couldn't be out in the sun for long periods of time. The more plastic surgery he did, took away the appearance of the young boy who kissed me on the beach that day. His life was changing as well as his looks.

Senior year, Peter had made several surprise visits in many different disguises. When he showed up in the library as a custodian, several times, my chemistry teacher, Mrs. Waters, caught him. She became our ally when he came to the school and allowed him to sit in on her lectures. Mrs. Waters was one of three teachers that let him go to class with me. And since other known famous people and students of known celebrities were in attendance, a "No Press" allowed on campus policy gave him freedom to visit.

Once the initial enthusiasm of him being on campus calm down, he enjoyed being out more. We went for walks some evenings. Ate in the cafeteria some afternoons and watched movies in the student lounge with other students. And Mrs. Waters was no joke too!

She said, "Since your here in my class you gotta work too!" She gave Peter assignments that he did and turned in. Wouldn't you know it, he got a B in that class. I got a B-. How do you like that!

The day of graduation, he was made an honorary grad and spoke at the ceremony. What he had to say was so profound that you thought he spent the whole 4yrs and then some there. As he took the podium to speak, you could feel the heart felt gratitude in his voice.

To even be up there in front of the students who worked so hard to become successful, made him humble in his words.

"Appreciative of showing me real hard work," he said applauding all the graduates from the podium.

He went on and spoke of life beyond our wildest dreams and accomplishment of things to come. Holding on to dreams and ambitions when the darkest comes in your pathway. Staying strong and steadfast through winter storms and floods of disappointments. The opportunity the school itself gave him to converse amongst them that year. A thing he will forever cherish. Something for him to hold on to in the times of distress he may come upon in his on personal journey that he could look back on as strength to overcome.

Peter went on as I sat there hanging on to every word with thoughts of his obstacles and life as I had known of it over those years. I felt so overcome with joy of his steadfast ability. He got his chance to see what it is to be like, common folks. It appeared as if he did get to make his escape from the glitz and glamor of the stardom life he had spoke of leaving once before the day we took that ride. His speech was motivating and I, so proud of him that day. Little did I know, the real escape was yet to come.

Chapter 10

By the time 1987 arrived, Bobby already had his degree in business management. He became a broker for Greg's trucking company and ran the fleet from the office and drove sometime. The trucks ran 48 states. They had a fleet of 15 trucks and growing before my last year in college. Greg continued to drive but not as much. His main focus was in the shop making sure the fleet kept rolling with very few engine problems.

Aunt B left that year also. She had been complaining of a head ache earlier one Sunday and laid down for her afternoon nap. When she woke up, she said she felt fine and drove herself to church like she always did for the first Sunday evening services. Sometime during the praise and worship session of service, she passed out. They thought she was just filled with the holy spirit. So, the deacons took her out to the nurses room to recover, like they do all folks who pass out, only to find she had gone on to glory. She had an unforeseen brain aneurism.

After working in a couple of clinics, I finally settled into a nursing position at the busiest hospitals in town. A multi-specialty academic level one medical trauma center known for skin graphing treatments and the highest recovery rate after second to third degree burns. There main force were on biomedical research and technologically. They had all the updated equipment, techniques and personnel to do the job. I was now following in moms footsteps.

As for the friendship with Peter, it was now being overcome by the unstoppable perils of adult hood. We knew that one day this was going to happen even though we tried not to let it. Both stayed so busy, there just wasn't time to spend together anymore. I'd call him but always got the machine. He'd send post cards sometime from exotic places but they were few and far in between. I kept most of them and framed my favorites. The friendship was still there but grown apart.

One night, I was asked to stay over to work a few hours until a nurse, who was running late came in. I had already been there since 6am and my feet were through. But I went ahead and stayed anyway to help out. They only needed me to stay long enough to administer the 10pm medicines and hang IV bags that needed changing. I had 4 rooms and 6 people to do. Mr. Addison was the last one then, I could take off.

When I entered the room with the cart, never did I look up to see the faces of the patients. Didn't want my tiredness to be seen in my eyes. Then, a voice from the chair beside the bed of Mr. Addison said, "Hi Minnie." To my surprise, it was Jack! I had not seen him in years and it was the best welcome of the evening.

I left the cart and gave him a big hug. But then stopped, backed away to see who he had came to visit. Laying in the bed with his eyes close wrapped in bandages around his head and face was Peter. He had been in a serious accident on a video shoot and obtain 3rd degree burns to his head. He had been admitted a few days prior but stayed in the intensive care unit. They moved him up stairs earlier in the day when a private room became available. Since I was not his incoming nurse, I never knew he was on the ward.

I moved in closer and touched his now very pale colored hand, "You are my star, that twinkles both day and by night," words I spoke from a poem he told me once. He opened his eyes surprised. I smiled and said, "Hi Peter."

His eyes soon turned cold. Jerking his hand away he said, "Go away! Get out of here! Leave me alone! Get out of my room!"

His reaction took me totally by surprise. I left with the cart fighting back the tears. I had heard this plenty of times from other patients. But this time, those words caught me off guard. We had known each other most of our lives and this was the response of a truly injured man. Injured in his pride, his public being and whatever else you could think of.

Jack followed me to the hallway. "Shelby, wait! He didn't mean it."

"I know he don't. It just caught me by surprise that's all," I said wiping a tear from my eye.

Jack gave one of his big brotherly hugs as he went on to tell what happened. "There was an explosion on the set with these fireworks and he got caught in the blast. He's been in a lot of pain."

"Don't worry, I'll look in on him from time to time," I said reassuring him.
"The staff here gives excellent patient care. He's in good hands."

With a slight smile he said, " Who would have thought that same little girl on a truck ride would grow up to be a great and pretty nurse. Look at you, Miss Shelby Johnson R.N."

"Didn't you know? I was always on my way here," I said trying to sound stuck up and hip but still the book worm he had known and loved like a little sister.

A few days past before I made another attempt to talk to Peter again. It was standard procedure to keep the charts updated daily on patients stay on the ward. I could monitor his chart everyday to see how his progress was coming. You can learn a lot from what the doctors, nurses, therapist and physiologist write on the patient. Peter was getting better everyday. But his medicines didn't look to be decreasing much at all. That could be a problem.

After my shift ended that Thursday, I went to his room. When I opened the door to peak in, he was sitting up watching television. He caught me! Waiting on the yells I got the last time, didn't come. Instead, he was overjoyed to see his old friend. He invited me in with that wonderful smile he always displayed. The playful Peter I had known and loved was back.

We talked for hours that evening about; whats been going on with me, what happened to him, where he's been, was I seeing anybody, where he's going. All the things, we hadn't had the chance to catch up on in our absence. It was like old times. I felt like Forest Gump when he said, "We were like peas and carrots again."

In the days to come, we got to spend late nights together. After visiting hours, I would take him on tours to see all the workings of the hospital. He needed to get out of the room and night was the best time for him without to many visitors around. We went by the MRI lab, the EKG room, Experimental studies, Xray room, just all over. He loved learning all about my new world of medicine and the staff loved showing him how it all worked. Every night a different ward or technical department.

There was a room that had a Hypodermic chamber machine. And like children, we just could not resist the opportunity to play Frankenstein. I slipped on a lab jacket and became the mad scientist and he jumped in the chamber to be Frankenstein. Faking like I was giving him life and he went right along with it coming to life in the machine. Little did we know that sometime later, someone had taken a picture and it hit the tabloids saying this was what he slept in every night to keep him youthful. As if he really was Peter Pan in the storybooks. Who would think of such a thing? How crazy was that?

On the last night of his stay, I had thought about everything we had shared. The good times, rough times, the laughter, the encounter, the pain and this was going to be our last adventure for a while. I knew he had concerns and very scared of his appearance. So I had one more place for him to visit. I wanted him to meet some special little people who themselves had been scared for life.

We went to a ward that had a multi-purpose room. Watching a magician, were a room filled with children. Peter squeeze my hand just a little tighter as his eyes surveyed the room while we stood at the back of the room. He wasn't afraid just sadden by what he saw. A few in specialty beds hooked to ventilators. Power chair children that move about by the touch of there heads. Some had artificial limbs and use walkers. Some had burn scares disfiguring their face. It was a room of heart felt pain that he never could imagine.

Once the magician was finish, nurse Debbie said, "OK, it's time for bed," they all sighed.

"Can we see one more trick, nurse Debbie, Please?" Keri, the child from the picture I received earlier in the story said. The other children urging on to her request.

"I'll tell you what," Peter said out loud. Letting go of my hand, he slowly walked to the front of the room, "If you all promise to go straight to bed, I'll come in and sing you a song. How about that?"

The light from their faces as they realized who he was made some of the biggest smiles ever. And their cheers was just the amount of medicine, he needed. They didn't care about his skin changing or the burn on his head. All they knew was a well known star had come to see them. They loved him for just being him. Pictures were taken in groups and individualize for some of them. In those few moments with them, changed his outlook on life forever. He had looked into the mirror of his life and decided, it was time for him to make a change.

Chapter 11

Being out on the open road for long periods of time, can get pretty tiresome when your at stretches of deserted areas. States like; Texas, New Mexico, Arizona and parts of California are really dull spots of seeing a whole lot of nothing. No cattle grazing in pastures, or horses running in fields. Mountains and Cactus are the usual sight. Places of deserted loneliness can really bring you back to times in your mind you'd like to forget.

****

At the prime old age of thirty something, Peter by now was married himself and started a family of his own. I married, a military man by the name of Dillon Robinson. Dillon was a Sargent at that time and was teaching on the Naval Base in Long Beach, California. He was 5'11ft with a lot of muscle and swagger about himself. A thing that caught everyone attention right off but I chose to ignore.

On the day we met, we were on the elevator together. He'd came to visit someone in the hospital along with some other military personnel. I was on my way back to the ward from EKG with a patient. He kept trying to make conversation but I made very short responses. When the elevator stopped at the floor, they got out too. Whoever they had come to see, was on my ward. This gave him more time to try and talk to me. I wasn't giving him the time of day.

After that first day, he started showing up for visits more and more. Trying to engage in conversations every time. The other nurses thought he was so attractive and I should at least here what he had to say. It wasn't that I didn't think he was fine and all. I just wasn't impressed. Work had become my knew best friend. I'd never given a thought to dating since Peter was married.

Long story short, we courted for some months before getting married. No major production, just went to the court house and did it there. The plan was to have a nice reception later but that never happened. We bought a house not that far from the base in Long Beach. I continued to work at the hospital and a nice life is what we had.

I talked to Peter a few times telling him all about everything. He was happy for me but as always, I could tell when there was more to it. I got the feeling, he didn't approve of Dillon based on what he had heard from a conversation between Jack and Bobby. The next thing I knew, we were in a heated argument over the phone. Said some pretty bad stuff to each other and never talk again. The friendship was over.

Two years into the marriage, I became pregnant with child at the same time Dillon was due to ship out overseas to do maneuvers in Lebanon for the next 6 months. The idea of starting a family was not in his plans. He didn't want children right away. Having a child would force him to wanna stay State side longer, which he did. He loved his work and just the two of us was all he wanted. A child would change all that.

I hated taking an aspirin so taking birth control pills was not the most desirable thing I wanted to do, but did. He never liked using a condom and didn't most of the time. He actually thought, I set him up. There are no guarantees with anything and he didn't understand that. By the time I was 8 months, Dillon was coming home drunk more and more starting arguments. I had enough of the verbal abuse and talked to dad earlier that day while at work. He was on the road at the time. I wanted to come home til the baby was born because of Dillon's behavior. But when I told Dillon of my plan, he wasn't having it!

The last day I ever saw him again was the night he came home drunk, loudly cursing me and the unborn child. He became more and more violent that night. Pushing and shoving me around saying, "You ain't going no where! You better not leave this house! You leave this house I'm gonna kill somebody!" Words that were sending chills through me.

After he took the car keys, I then began to call my brother Bobby on the house phone to come get me right now. Dillon snatched the phone out of the wall and threw it across the room yelling. His rage was terrifying, grabbing me by the neck, slammed me into a wall face first almost knocking me out. Dillon then picked me up by the hair like a caveman and dragged me to the bedroom unbuckling his belt.

He dropped me to the floor and pulled the belt from his waist. I thought he was gonna beat me with it. Instead, he tied my wrist together behind my back and pushed me to the bed. Then, he left the room briefly. Cries to untie me, fell upon deaf ears. Dillon was making me a prisoner in our own home. I never saw him like this.

As I laid there face first in the comforter, I could hear his footsteps coming back to the room. Vision just slightly blurred, I watched him at the doorway guzzling down yet another beer. I tired to get up but a cramping pain started to overcome me. Seeing my struggle, he came over to the bed and sat on my back to ensure a get away was inevitable. Dillon didn't care about the pain but I knew something was seriously wrong with the baby.

Once he felt the strength of my escape had subsided, he then got up ripping my cloths off. Throwing them everywhere around the room until I was completely bare. Picking back up the bottle he sat on the floor, he stood me up and held me close to him with my hands still tied to weak to run. The smell the liquor from his breath was stronger then ever as he licked the tears from my face and took a swig from the bottle. The pain once again had become greater but he still wouldn't listen. An urge that was throbbing in his pants needed a quick fix. It had his full attention and no baby was going to defer him from that.

The yelling cries of pain went on at least an hour or so with no signs of stopping. The harsh slaps he gave to silence me as the pain grew more and more as he forced himself inside. Blood began to run out onto the comforter with every drive. Still he would not stop. After all that had been done, I knew now why the pain was so horrifying. Finally, I passed out.

After weeks in the hospital, I was released. I didn't file a report but I heard that Bobby and Jack made a late night visit to the house one night. Who knows what happened. Dillon left the country with the troops and filed for the divorce before leaving. He gave me the house but I didn't care to live there. I didn't even care about work at the hospital anymore. Phone calls, visits, letters, television anything that was connected to the outside world had become lost. Peter tried to contact me as well. I didn't want to be bothered by him either.

Dad brought me home to my old bedroom at Aunt B's house. I spent most of my recovery time sitting quietly in the room, reading books or just looking out the window. It had become my new interest. Months went by until my dad had a heart to heart talk with me. Let me tell you! Daddy's know everything! Even when you don't think they aren't paying attention, Oh they know! He knew exactly what I felt.

It was a place he'd been living in for years now since Nadine passed away. How he felt when they told him, Will was never coming home. Never being able to see his own son or kiss his wife ever again. A feeling of complete pain and solitude. A closet you never want to come out of or see sun light. A place, I had found refuge in being.

"Shelby," he said. "You are my only daughter and I love you. It's ok to get mad at someone for what they say or do. People will always try to find ways to bruise your soul. You have a wonderful heart just like your mother. You give and love much better then I ever could. Don't let the wrongs of one man cloud your judgment of another who still loves you and never stopped."

He took a book off the bookshelf across the room and sat it on the bed. It was the story, I had read to mom and gave to my best friend. My favorite children story, "The Prince and the Pauper." Then for the first time, my dad, my hero, the man I always leaned on over the years began to weep. He understood more things then I could ever imagine. He loved me and felt bad enough he wasn't here to protect me at the time.

****

It's now as of today, over 40 yrs ago since Nadine left that April. My dad, Greg, left due to Prostate Cancer at a rip old age of 73years old the same year I got in a truck to start a life of truck driving."I miss them both!"

Chapter 12

It had been a long ride coming down Hwy 40 to get to the California border. And as usual the slow down once again was at the Agricultural Station near Lake Havasu. It didn't matter what you were pulling you had to stop and get questioned by the officers before continuing. This was the first time, I ever came through in the night and it went much faster.

Just past the station was another truck stop. It would be my last shut down to rest before pulling into the mortuary. The main problem was finding a place to park amongst the sea of trucks already there. The later you arrive at a well known truck stop, the chances of finding a parking space was slim to none. Many drivers park on the on ramps or on the shoulder of the highway. A very dangerous place to be. The likelihood of another truck or car running into you was scarier then you could ever imagine. Not the smartest place for a truck to be. So, I took the time to find a safe place to park on the lot.

Somewhere along the way, I made up time and would be there early in the afternoon for the delivery to Forest Lawn. Afterward, I would park the big white 53ft truck and trailer at the yard and finally go home to my bathtub. Showers are alright sometime but a sit 'n soak wins out every time. That's what I wanted the most!

As I laid in the back in the bunk, I turned on the television to see what was the latest on the news. But instead, a movie caught my attention. It was, The American Dream. A movie I had at home in my collection. I'd seen it over a dozen times but watched it anyway. It wasn't before long, it was watching me. Drifting into slumber, I dreamed about something no one in the world ever knew about me and Peter. It was the biggest secret we had with each other. The paparazzi would have a field day if they only knew. Shh! It's a secret!

****

It was the winter after Greg died I took a load out on the truck to New York City. The city was covered in the wintery frost. What a beautiful sight. It had snowed earlier that day and was due for more before night fall. I was carrying a load of seats that were being installed on the ground floor level of the famous Madison Square Garden. It was going to take the rest of the afternoon to unload due to limited room.

When I arrived and backed into there docks, I went right away inside to do the paperwork while the workers unloaded the freight. Since it was gonna take a while I did my usual thing of noising around the building. It was the most amazing auditorium I had ever been in. I wound up on the big stage this time and was astonished at the view. It was like, WOW!

"I remember the first time I stood right where your standing thinking the same thing," an unexpected voice said from the wings. "It is pretty incredible. Just like you."

A tall light skin man in a white wool trench p-coat and scarf, wearing a black suit and tie underneath walked slowly in my direction caring a single rose. He pushed his hat up on his head so his face could then be revealed. Wouldn't you just know it! It was Peter. We had not talked since that day on the phone. And now, here he stood with the same warm smile I met over 20 years ago.

"Hi Minnie," he said coming closer. "You are one hard lady to catch up with."

"How did you know I was here?" I said, then stopped. "Bobby!"

"I needed to see you," he said. "I heard about your dad. He was a good man and father. I'll miss him too. But most of all, I miss our friendship and all the great times we shared together."

"Yeah, but...." I started to say.

"….Forget about the past," he said cutting my speech short and handing the rose. "Nothing else matters right now."

I nearly forgot that Jack and Bobby were still the best of friends and they always talked. Peter had been up to speed on everything that went on in my life. They all knew how bad the painful life with Dillon had left me. Peter understood most of all but never would I take his calls. Bobby thought it would be a great idea if Peter would pay a surprise visit. Hoping to put our friendship back in it's proper place. Something even my dad, Greg wanted to see done.

Taking my wrist slightly pulling up the sleeve of my jacket, "I see, you still have it." He spoke of the beaded bracelet he gave me years ago. I pulled away. "I knew you still thought about me, cause I still thought about you," he then said almost rejoicing at the thought.

I didn't know what to say. Apart of me was glad, then another part was ready to fall into his arms and cry, and yet another part was mad at the last conversation. But for the record, I went for part two and fell into his arms. He held me close and tight in his arm just like the night of the dance.

I said sadly,"I missed you too."

Pausing he said, "I know this little deli down the street. They have the greatest hot chocolate." He thought it was a much more better atmosphere then the stage. A place we never shared in the first place. And so, away we went.

Once at the deli, we sat and talked like old times again. He did most of the talking and the hot cocoa was great! He told me of his adventures and marriages. He already knew about my disastrous life so there wasn't to much to say. He had two children and sole custody. Peter loved being their father. It made him grow up in so many ways. I was glad for him but sad for myself. I still had no children nor a love of my own.

Then he said something that would change our lives forever. Leaning over close, he whispered softly, "I've been in love with you since the first time we kissed on the beach that summer. I promise, I will never hurt you or make you cry." Singing his next line, "..♫.Cause, I just can't stop...♪.lovin' you. Shelby Johnson Robinson, will you marry me?"

What did he just say!? What was I to say? Had he just lost his mind? What was he thinking? Is this a Bobby joke or something? Where are the hidden cameras? What kind of life was I about to have being married to a superstar? Is this some kind of crazy dream? I closed my eyes real tight for a long time.

"What are you doing?" Peter said.

"Trying to wake up from this crazy dream," I said.

Laughing, he placed his warm soft hand to my face gently and said, "It's not a dream. I'm very real."

Slowly, I opened my eyes to look into his gleaming eyes. I could tell he spoke words of truth about his request. After all the years of hitting and missing at each other, my best friend asked me to share his wonderful exotic life of adventure with him. I never thought these words would ever come my way. He was the one steady love I ever had in my life but would this joining mess up our relationship or enhance it?

Just as I was about to speak, the cell phone in his pocket rang. At first he ignored it to wait for my answer. I was a little lost for words and told him to answer it, which he did. A million thoughts went running at once through my mind. Most of all, I was flattered by his offer. But from the sound of his voice, the conversation over the phone distracted my thoughts any further. It sounded serious. When he got off, he said he had to leave right away.

We wasted no time rushing back to the Garden. The limo was waiting door open, engine running. I fell back in my steps to watch him depart. But just as he was about to get in the car, he stopped and came back.

"Come with me Minnie," he said. "Share my life with me as my wife. We are forever."

"I'm sorry Peter. I can't do it," I said. "It's not that I don't love you. You are to famous now and that's not the kind of life I'm ready for."

I could see what was said cut him very deeply but he didn't press the issue. He said not a word. Then with a flash, he was in the car and whisked away leaving me with his words of love ringing in my ears and a single rose. Every thing I had been through over the past years had come to this moment. A moment that I was going to let slip by and for what?

"WHAT AM I CRAZY!?"

I ran back to the truck which was still being unloaded and dropped the trailer. I had to catch that limo before he got to the plane at JFK Airport and in the snow that wasn't going to be easy. I didn't bother with chains just used the 4 wheel drive gauge on the truck console to ensure I made proper stops when needed. Not what you suppose to do but can.

When I finally reached the airport, the limo driver was getting back into the car. I parked the truck in the middle of traffic to get out and stopped him. He had taken Peter straight on the field to his jet. I had missed him by 5 minutes. Then, the driver gave me a letter he was instructed to bring back from Peter. He had picked up another client and was about to do that when I arrived. I thanked him and started back toward the truck opening the letter along the way.

It read:
Do you remember the time we first met.
We fell in love, so young and innocent then.
How it all began, seemed like heaven, didn't want it to end. Us holding hands and staring into each others eyes.
We used to talk, stayed on the phone night til dawn.
Walks in the park and on the beach. Those sweet memories will always hold dear to me. And no matter what you say I will never forget what we had. I will never let you go. Not ever again. We are forever.

Chapter 13

We had kept our lives a secret from the public for many years by 2002. And after a very long courtship, I once again was expecting a child. This time from a man who really loved me. We weren't married yet but loved each other very much. Everyone close to us was very happy about the news. Mr. J was not in agreement with us having a child out of wed-lock but there wasn't much he could do or say. There were other issues being faced at the Havenhurst house that he was involved in like liquidating funds for tax reasons!

Peter had bought the biggest house on a piece of land that stretched out as far as 20 city blocks. 580 acres of land in the Santa Barbara area. It was equipped with a studio, theater, petting zoo, and amusement park rides. All the things he loved so well. To me, it was like living in a luxury castle style prison. Most of the time, he and the children were over my Aunt B. house. I never moved out of it again since the thing with Dillon.

Oh yeah, although I never saw Dillon again, I heard Dad and Bobby talking about him one day long ago. They said, he was at some club partying with officers somewhere in Liberia and masked men burst in with guns and took him. No one claim to know why they just targeted him. But when they found his body weeks later, he was naked and badly dehydrated from the sun tied to a tree in the desert. Karma! Now that I think back, Peter sent me a postcard around the same time from there. He was in the area on tour or something like that. I forget. Hum, I wonder!?

Anyway, lawyers had Peter in and out of court on some of the most unreal causes and dragging me into it was not what he wanted to do. I kept on truck driving and stayed on the road til I couldn't. Keeping out of sight from the press, we met in secret places and he made late night visits with the children when I was home. He even hired a look alike to appear in places pretending to be him just to get away. Some looked exactly like him. But after the trail was over, he slipped it out about another child coming into his life at a press conference.

Telling reporters, "Now since the courts have found no cause to detain me for the hideous crimes the prosecution had allegedly accused me of, I plan to reside home with family anxiously awaiting the arrival of my third child due any day now."

The story was, a surrogate woman had been artificially in-simulated and caring this child. The cameras followed him every where trying to get a glimps of the mother. But they were unsuccessful in there search. Peter had kept his own children identity a mystery from the world. He didn't want them to grow up not being able to escape the public like himself.

Peter stayed at the castle with the kids and worked on another album. If you ever really listen to the lyrics, you could always tell what was happening in his life. Love, violence in the world, drugs, invading his privacy, even parts of our relationship were set to music. A couple of the songs were directed to the paparazzi for all the abuse they put his career through. All the hard work and good will he did was becoming lost in the controversy.

The trail really took a toll on him emotionally. He wasn't sleeping much and rehearsed continuously without rest. I really started worrying about him more and more. He was considering retiring soon. But on the day Miguel arrived, I discovered by accident what was keeping him going.

Peter wrote me lovely poems in the past that he later put to music. That night while we were in the studio at the castle house recording one of the poems, Peter and the engineering crew worked on the song for the next album. I wasn't feeling well. Using his bag for a pillow and coat for a cover, I laid down on the little couch in the recording room close to him.

"Are you alright," he asked covering me with the coat.

"Yeah, I'm good," I lied. "But when you get done, I'd really like to have some of those famous french toast you make."

"This will be the last take guys," he announced walking back to the mic.

His voice was always so soothing when the discomforts of being pregnant over ran me. Luckily, this was a slow song and felt real soothing. But as I laid there listening, I just couldn't get comfortable. The bag that served as a pillow fell to the floor and out spilled pill bottles. Vicodin, Morphine, Demoral were just a few.

The look on my face of anger as I picked up the bottles and read them caused Peter to cut the session short and dismissed everyone. I said not a word and went back up to the main living area of the house to get my coat to just leave. He knew how much I didn't like the idea of him taking pills and promised to stop. He claimed he only needed them sometime but he had become addicted. As the discussion began to escalate, a pain hit and my water broke. Peter called the doctor.

We didn't make it to the hospital that night. Miguel was born right there at the house, 7lbs 21oz and had a head full of soft black hair. We called him Pillow. He was the most wonderful thing I had ever seen. Sitting beside me on the bed holding me and the baby, Peter made a vow to get help and promised to stop the addiction. A promise, he did not break. He was now once again a very proud father. And as the leader of his family, he knew he had to set a better example.

The rest of our family and friends came to the house later that next day. Mr. J even had his chest stuck out a little. Bobby and Jack, with their new families, making plans to teach him how to play ball. And the beautiful Ms. Anita Knight came by to wish us well. She also kept in touch over the years. The children loved having another little person to watched over and play with.

As I looked out the window from the bed I was now confined to, the sun seemed a little bit brighter. And during all the expressed display of love and affection from everyone, all I could do was wish Nadine and Greg were here to see their grandson. Smothering him with kisses. Aunt B baking him some cookies just as she did when we were kids. Some how I felt they were looking down on us with a smile. And their love was shinning on us.

****

I arrived at the mortuary 2 hours earlier then was proposed but it was alright with the manager Mr. Smith. He wanted to give the workers a short day anyway so it worked out good for all. As they were unloading, I went to find a restroom. Turning a corner, I literally ran into Jack and fell to the floor. It was always so good to see him but not from this position.

"I'm so sorry Minnie," he said helping me up off the floor. "Are you alright?"

"Yeah, I'm good," I said wiping my back side. "I'd been trying to call the house."

"It's been really crazy around there and all over town," he said. "Bobby said he talked to you a few days ago."

"He did," I said sadly. "He's here isn't he?"

"Down the hall. Mr. J is there now," he said. "We came down to check the final arrangements and the casket. Mr. Smith special ordered one due in on the truck today."

"I just backed in and they are unloading now. Jack, how are....." I began to say.

"....They are fine, and at my house for now," he said.

Then a familiar voice called out to Jack from down the hall. It was Mr. J. Wasn't in a hurry to see him! He always looked at me as if I was the enemy. But this time, he did something that surprised me. He came over and gave the biggest hug and said, "Shelby." I was without words.

"You have been my sons friend for so long, I can't remember. Blessed our family with life that makes everyone smile," he said. "You two got into more things then I wanted and if I was your father you'd caught a beaten too.

But you stayed true and that's rare in a world of gimme folks. I know you loved him cause he loved the hell out of you. I'm glad your here and I just wanted to tell you myself, Thank you."

Now here was a strong stern man who I just knew hated my guts saying something that had me dumb founded. He then went back down the hall and out of the front doors never looking back. Leaving me with this look of shock on my face, Jack gave more clarity on his behavior. You see, he cared for me more then he wanted to show. He acted the same way toward all of his children as well. I had been around so long now, I was one of them.

Mr. Smith came through with paperwork for Jack and I. It was back to the business at hand. Jack gave me all the info for the service tomorrow and hoped I would say something at the services. He wanted me to come to the house later but I just explained how long I had been gone. As the big brother I had known him to be, he understood. It was going to be a private service so I would still be safe out of the sights of the medias view.

Apart of me had to see him before leaving the building. I still felt like this was a bad dream. Jack saw my hesitating steps.

"It's the second door on the left," Jack said before going back to Mr. Smith office. "You need me to go with you?"

"No, Been a long ride. I will see you tomorrow," I said walking back the other way. Abandoning the original quest for the bathroom and the thought of seeing my beloved Peter like that, I just couldn't do it.

Chapter 14

I still lived in the home of my Aunt B over on 107th and Figueroa in South Central Los Angeles, California but by myself. The neighborhood is not so innocent as it was back in the days when Bobby and Jack played basketball in the drive. The make shift net still hung over the garage door. Bars were on every window and a security door on the front and back of the house. Often when I came home, Peter would make his arrival at the front door with the children. And once again the house was filled with laughter. Now going home would be not as joyful knowing his body now rested else where instead of with me tonight.

Once inside the house, I checked the machine to hear messages about CNN news. I quickly shut it off. I then went to the bathroom to start the water and returned to the kitchen to grab something to eat. All the while of my travels through the house remembering the boy who grew to a man that shared space there with me more times then one could count. And the children that came later filling the house with sounds of family.

After the hot food and bath, I laid in the covers we shared only a few weeks ago. His scent still lingered in the bed linens. I wrapped the blankets around my body as if he was there holding me tightly like he use to. Faced down in them, I took a deep breath trying to engulf myself with his faint presents that still lived on in them.

I looked up to the night stand at a post card of a beautiful waterfall some where in the country side of Liberia. He had sent it years ago and I framed it. Taking it out to read what he wrote on the sending side, just one word, "Neverland." I cried for my wonderful parents. I cried for my sweet Aunt. I cried when the unborn child was lost. I cried for myself at the hurt Dillon pressed upon me. But tonight, I cried harder than ever for a love that was no longer in my reach. My love was gone much to soon.

****

After the last of the two trails, Peter sold the castle and rented an apartment style mansion in Westwood, California. He had gotten the help that was needed to stop the addiction from growing worse. 7 years clean. His health was good. His mind and soul was more at one. But age has a way of catching up to you when you least expect it. Body aches were more common but he had a therapist for that, to work out the kinks. A private doctor kept an account of all prescribed drugs administered to him, and often traveled with him. He maintained keeping his promise to me and that made our love even stronger.

The media witch hunt was every where. Anything he did was under scrutiny. The police and private investigators were raiding his life and homes. Dragging his career through the mud. I personally thought that when a second trail came about heading the same allegations as the last, appeared to be somewhat of a conspiracy to try and break him. They questioned many of his friends for months. The doctor was also closely watched and questioned often. I can't say that I trusted him much. Hmm, I wonder did they put him up to something?

Peter talked more and more of retiring from the business and marriage as well. We planned on having the ceremony during the tour. There was one more album of music he wanted to get out. He had spent his whole life on the stage but now he just wanted the peaceful life I had shown him over the years in my home. But there was something else he wasn't saying. I could feel it way down deep inside. So like always, I didn't force it and waited for him to say just as he always did in the past. But this time, he never said a word.

I had pretty much stopped truck driving. The company Bobby and my dad, Greg, started had now become a major trucking company on the west coast. But still, there were times when he needed my help with some of our regular dedicated accounts, like the Evansville Casket Company.

I was the boss' daughter and had a good repore with the company CEO. This was the ride, I had just came in from.

Our last night together was at my house. Peter had just tucked the kids into bed in my old room. Sang them there special song to put them to sleep, then came into the room that I now slept in that was Aunt B's, and fell onto the bed next to me. He had been rehearsing dancers and putting the show together over the past 3 months. It was just about ready to go.

The tour was set to start in London and tour all over parts of Europe over the summer. The news reported that once the venues were set for the tour, tickets sold out in less then a week. Peter made the announcement at a press conference saying, "This is it. The last tour. I am officially retiring."

At 50yrs old, he felt the time had come.

Myself and the children were going with him this time. The children had always been to little to experience what he did for a living and he wanted to give them a special treat. I never went to any of his tours either so it was gonna be a treat for me as well.

Both laying side by side staring at the ceiling, he began doing that thing he does with his mouth (Beat Box) using me as a snare. It always made me laugh when he did it. Then still keeping the beat going he began to sing.

"♪♪..I like the way how you holding me, ♪..I like the way how you loving me. I like how you touching me, ♪..I like the way how you kissing me, ♪..You see, It won't be long til we make vows, ♪♪..I thank the heavens above that I met ya. ♪..I was alone there wasn't love in my life, ♪♪..I was afraid of loving, you came in time, ♪..You took my hand we kissed in the moonlight, ♪..Ooo"

He sung another round of it pulling me along rocking side to side. No matter how tired he was, the creativity in him would not rest even in bed. He was always the ray of sunshine in my life. Now, we were finally sharing moon beams of love together. I didn't ever want this to end.

He stopped singing, "Minnie, I can't sleep." Suddenly serious, "I never wanted for anything as bad as I want this."

I thought he was talking about the tour and all that goes with it. So I said,
"You have nothing to worry about. Your fans have loved you from the day you stepped in front of a mic 30 years ago til now."

He turned over and looked at me with the same seriousness, "I'm not talking about the tour. I mean us. Our family. Our life. You and the children mean so much to me. I don't want to miss being with you all by being out there like that. "

"We love you too and even if you decided to stay out there in the business, we'd be right beside you," I said reassuring him.

"But you know, there isn't any real escape from the fame you achieved. You are a great man, a legend, an icon, a wonderful father, a beautiful spirit, a humanitarian, a master of your craft, the greatest son, brother and best friend. Loved by people young and old all over the world. Something that big can't just walk away."

I got up and went to the closet to pull out the bag I was gonna take for the ride I was about to go on in the truck. I had to get an early start but had not put a bag together yet. Peter didn't like that I was going on the ride but he understood how I felt about keeping Greg's dream alive as much as I could. He would do the same. But Peter made me stop packing to continue our conversation by sitting me down on the bed.

Then he knelt down holding my hand sliding a ring on my finger requesting my hand in marriage the proper way. My heart almost jumped out of my chest at the site of this 20kt diamond rock on a platinum band. It was the most beautiful thing I had ever seen. I was so happy.

"I want to make it official this time," he said. "Will you marry me?"

I began to cry saying, "Yes." Peter took me in his arms comfortingly and I forgot all about the bag and the tour.

That night was the most magical moment of love. It felt like the day I got that autograph picture from Ms. Anita Knight. The grooviest thing of all time! We danced around the room humming the tune of, Here Comes the Bride. I don't know who was more excited, me or him.

Well, I ain't got to tell you what went down after that. I'm sure by now you would have guessed. But I will say, if there was any thought of us making any more children, that night it was sure to happen!

Chapter 15

It was a warm evening on the lawn at the cemetery where everyone was seated in white chairs near the mausoleum. The press were not invited and all the who is who of Hollywood was there. The famous Staple Center held a memorial earlier that day for the fans and had a spectacular array of celebrities speak there as well. They rendered songs and reflections to commemorate the man that changed the world by song at the service and the arena. It was beautiful. As for me, I felt like my father did many years ago when they buried my mother. I just want this day to be over already. I didn't want to be here.

I thought back at all the fun we shared as many spoke of him at the service. A time when we wanted to just run away from the world and enjoy places like Disneyland everyday of our lives. A thought of the hurt we endured through others and how bouncing back together made us happy. Discovering life and love in places one couldn't tell anybody about. And now all of that, would just be a fond memory to keep locked away in mind and heart, forever.

We laid him to rest that night in a well secured place the public would never be allowed to visit. The thought of some crazy nut out there digging up his remains and selling it like, they tried to do to the famous Charlie Chaplin was something the family wasn't about to endeavor. We didn't have a traditional repast like most. The public was having there own all over town for days prior and after. The family just greeted all the friends there at the service and called it a day. It didn't end til almost 10pm that night.

After everything was over weeks and weeks later, the crowds of people who flooded the city were now heading back to their lives all over the world. The press was so involved with the doctor and his part of the death. The will and who would get custody of the kids, seemed more of what everyone wanted to know. Mr. J being the leader of the family would only let the press have some of the inside scoop. It wasn't his thing to let to many people into there family life.

While all of that was happening, I and the children took a ride down to the Hollywood Walk of Fame to see all the gifts left at the star. And to make the delivery, I had promised. The store in front of the star was over ran by cards posters, teddy bears and stuff. The store owner came out as we stood there reading some of the posters.

He told us of all the people around the world that had come to this place. And all the things there would be picked up sometime that day and sent over to the family. He didn't recognize the children. Peter kept them well hidden from the public too as they grew up. He just thought we were some left over fans.

"We wanna see," Pillow said to the man.

"I'm sorry, sir we will be moving on shortly," I said.

He then went back inside his store satisfied with my answer. I then reached into my pocket and pulled out the napkin which held the gift from Carol the waitress at the diner. The cross with the inscription and the picture from the lady on the bus ride who became sick. Her deceased daughter Keri, a burn patient. I placed them both in a spot on the star.

"Those were nice gifts you brought," a voice from behind said.

"It was from people who I met along the way trying to get here," I said never turning around.

"They must have been big fans. And you as well to do something for strangers," he said.

"My daddy said never talk to strangers," Pillow came right out and said.

The man gave a slit chuckle and some how it was very familiar. I then turned around. There stood a tall lighter shade of brown skin man. His hair cut short and slightly frosted on the sides. He looked to be in his early 50ties wearing a polo shirt and slacks with tennis shoes.

He was part of the crew to pick up the things left at the star the store owner talked about. Nice looking but wasn't any one I knew.

"Please forgive my son, he can be very honest a lot of times," I said.

"A child who truly listens to his father," he smiled and said. Bending down to Pillows level, "Young man, only you would ever know the success of true freedom."

His words took me totally by surprise. I had only heard those words in a conversation once years ago by the steps of George Washington High School. A topic headed off about the story of the Prince and the Pauper and how it was possible. How Peter himself thought he could just pull it off. A conversation that I had long since forgotten about until this day.

Could it? Did he really fix his appearance so nobody really knew who he was now? Was the body in the casket, one of the clones who wanted to be him? Or was I just imagining who I wanted him to be?

"Come on kids, we got to get out of these people way," I told the kids as we began walking back in the direction of the car with the stranger following us.

"Hey don't leave. I think it's great you brought the children to see such a fantastic display of out pouring," he said.

His voice was soothing as he spoke. It had such a calming effect about it. I turned to see him close at hand. Apart of me had to look into his eyes. I had to see. "Thank You. I'm sorry but aren't you here to pick up all this stuff?" I said coming just a little closer to look at him.

"Yes," he said with a smile. "Better get back to work," turns to leave.

"Hey, wait," I said. "I didn't catch your name."

"It's daddy, daddy, daddy, daddy," Pillow said jumping up and down.

"Stop it Miguel," I fussed.

He slowly turned back around looking down at fidgety child I had a hold of.
"Funny, you can't hide anything from children," he said with a smirk. "They can see what no one else can, or won't."

He then reached out to shake my hand. I took it as a regular form of greeting at first. But before I could say anything, he said, "My name is Addison and I already know who you are."

At that moment, it was as if I was back on the beach in Atlantic City on the blanket under the umbrella when I was 10yrs. The sounds of the world stopped once again. The cars swooshing by, passer byres chatting away could not be heard. I never saw this man before but yet he was known in my heart. The warmth of his hand felt familiar and nice. His soothing tone voice made the hairs on the back of my neck tickle. The smile in his eyes spoke the truth of what Pillow, so easily shouted out. Could it really be?

"Peter?" I asked hesitating.

And with a smile, he said, "Hello, Minnie."

"And With This End, We Start A New Begin."
Shh!

EPILOGUE

Dear Peter,

Hold my Hand for I wanna be where you are. Never can say goodbye because I Got to be there. A simple question of Who's lovin' you, finds the answer that You are my life. She drives me wild, this thief of life. The girl is mine, Can't let her get away to the beat Ben does with Billie Jean. Will you be there to see the Blood on the dance floor that came Much to soon?

Invincible wonderful joy you've given, let all the world know Who is it that unfolds these reflections of Black or white. My heart skips a beat so filled by your love. I Keep the faith everyday, only you Rock my world.

Say, say, say, the Stranger in Moscow spoke, One day in your life I'll take you on the Carousal of Unbreakable joy. Cry or Scream on this Thriller ride and watch out, for that Speed Demon coming with that latest Breaking news. Leave me alone! Tabloid Junkies, Working day and night are but Smooth criminals on a mission to bruise the heart.

Gone to soon our happiness of Human nature, find myself pleading don't Fly away. I just cant stop loving you. I like the way you love me. Butterflies deep within my soul makes me Speechless, The way you make me feel.

*You've always been my **Best of joy. I can't make it another day** without your touch. Stay! **Baby be mine.** Forever **The lady in my life, Girlfriend,** that **PYT,** is all I ever wanted to be.*

*   **This time around** I'll take the lead **Behind the mask** to run the **Monster** far away. So **Keep your head up** to the **Break of dawn,** even though **Heaven can't wait, You are not alone. They don't care about us** but **Don't walk away,** for **Whatever happens** the **Earth song** will ring on. **The lost children** need us to continue to **Heal the world** and save lives. And as we have been all these years, **Just good friends** together forever, **This is it** making the difference.*

*   I ask of them **Why you wanna trip on me,** invading the righteous of our **Privacy?** Hopes and dreams we share exploited by those who **Don't stop til you get enough. Give into me,** 'cause you **Wanna be startin' somethin', Heartbreaker, Dirty Diana?** Your **Streetwalker** days are over and done. So long to **The Liberian girl,** and **Beat it,** she did.*

*   Then **Another part of me** looked at that **Man in the mirror** and suddenly became sadden by the shattered sight of the **Dangerous, Bad, Off the wall, Jam** of the **Morphine** pieces that **Rock with you.** Freed from the nightmare, of the **Hollywood night,** a new adventure was about to begin. So, **I Can't help it** when **2000 watts** of explosive love burst from hiding **In the closet.** The **Someone in the dark** feels no longer **Threaten** like in our **Childhood** enchanted life. Never will we ever forget and forever we will always **Remember the times.***

Love Minnie